Shortcut
Donald Crews

Watercolor and gouache paints were used for the full-color art. An airbrush was used for accents. The text type is Futura Bold Italic.

ISBN 0-590-97545-5

Copyright © 1992 by Donald Crews. All rights reserved. Published by Scholastic Inc., 555 Broadway, New York, NY 10012, by arrangement with Greenwillow Books, a division of William Morrow & Company, Inc. TRUMPET and the TRUMPET logo are registered trademarks of Scholastic Inc.

12 11 10 9 8 7 6 5 4 3 2 1
6 7 8 9/9 0 1/0

Printed in the U.S.A.

To Mama/Daddy

Brother/Shirley
Mary
Sylvester/Edward
Sylvia

All's well
that
ends well

We looked....
We listened....
We decided to take
the shortcut home.

We should have taken the road.
But it was late, and it was
getting dark, so we
started down the track.

We knew when the passenger trains passed. But the freight trains didn't run on schedule. They might come at any time.

We should have taken the road.

WHOO-WHOO

The track ran along a mound.
Its steep slopes were covered
with briers. There was
water at the bottom, surely
full of snakes.

We laughed. We shouted. We sang.
We tussled. We threw stones.
We passed the cut-off that
led back to the road.

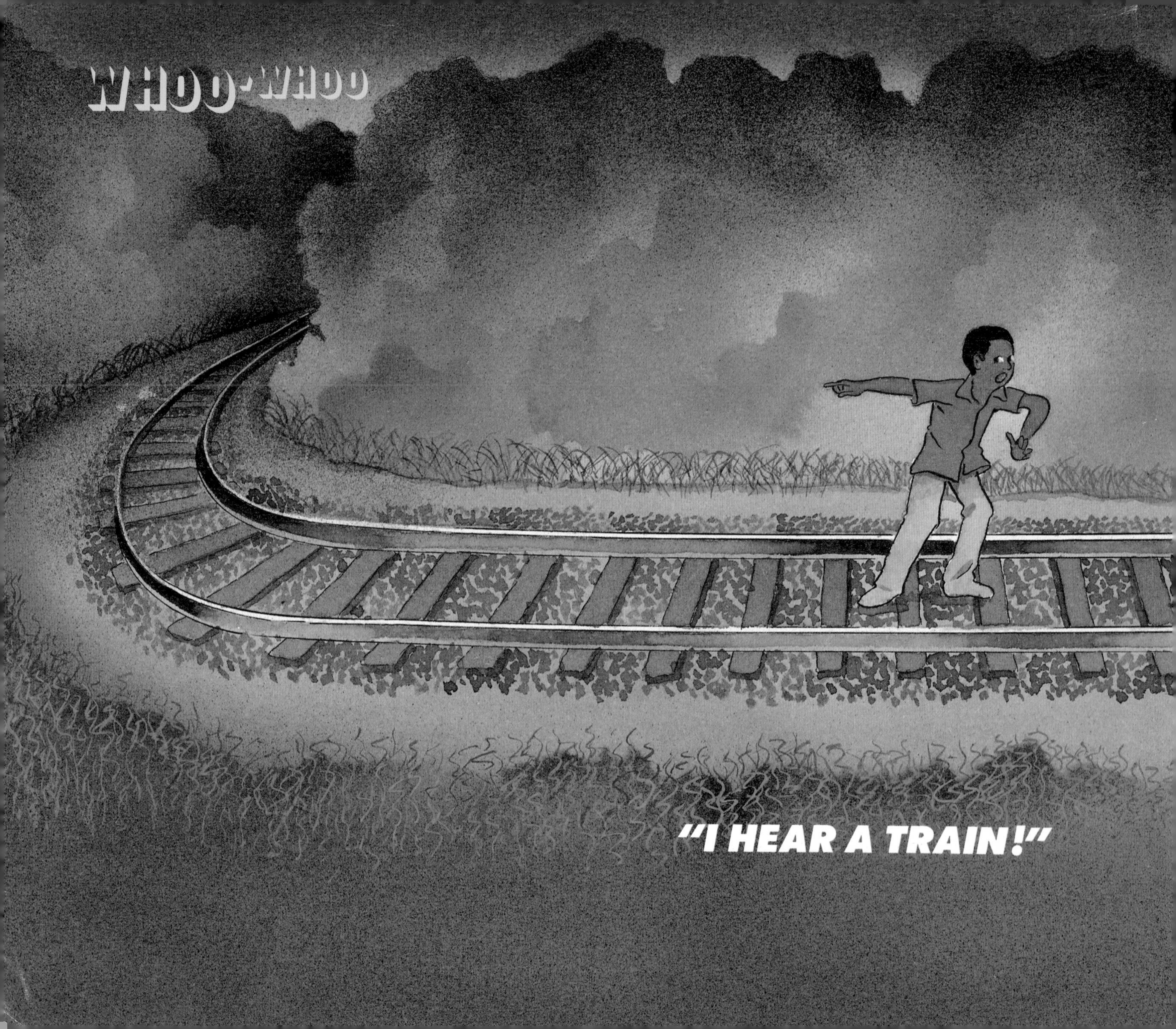

"I HEAR A TRAIN!"

Everybody stopped.   *We all heard the train whistle.*
Everybody listened.   *Should we run ahead to the*
            path home or back to the cut-off?

WHOO

The train whistle was much louder.

WHOO

WHOO

We jumped off the tracks onto the steep slope. We didn't think about the briers or the snakes

KLAKITY-KLAK-KLAK

KLAK, KLAKITY

KLAKITY-KLAK

KLAK KLAKITY

KLAKITY-KLAK-KLAK

The train passed.
We were all fine.
We climbed back onto the tracks.
We hurried to the cut-off
and onto the road.

*We walked home without a word.
We didn't tell Bigmama. We didn't tell Mama.
We didn't tell anyone. We didn't talk about
what had happened for a very long time.
And we didn't take the short-cut again.*